Superphonics *Storybooks* **will help your child to learn to read using Ruth Miskin's highly effective phonic method. Each story is fun to read and has been carefully written to include particular ~~~ds and spellings.**

The Storybooks are graded~~~~~~~~~ progress with confidence fr~~~~~~~~~ras to harder ones. There are four levels - Blue (the easiest), Green, Purple and Turquoise (the hardest). Each level is linked to one of the core *Superphonics Books*.

ISBN 0 340 77351 0

Text copyright © 2001 Gill Munton
Illustrations copyright © 2001 Clive Scruton

Editorial by Gill Munton
Design by Sarah Borny

The rights of Gill Munton and Clive Scruton to be identified as the author and illustrator of this Work have been asserted by them in accordance with the Copyright, Designs and Patents Act 1988.

First published in Great Britain 2001

10 9 8 7 6 5 4 3 2 1

First published in 2001 by Hodder Children's Books, a division of Hodder Headline Limited, 338 Euston Road, London NW1 3BH

Printed by Wing King Tong, China

A CIP record is registered by and held at the British Library.

Target words

This Purple Storybook focuses on the following sounds:

ay as in **play** | **a-e** as in **game**
ai as in **snail** | **ey** as in **they**

These target words are featured in the book:

away	amazing	late	shame
awayday	Ape	latest	shape
bay	brake	made	skate
day	case	mate	boards
holiday	chase	mistake	take
may	Crazy	page	takes
okay	escape	pale	
pay	face	parade	afraid
play	fame	place	again
runaway	game	plane	brained
says	gape	plate	chains
stay	gate	race	fail
today	Jake	rage	gains
way	Jake's	rate	Grail
	lake	sake	paid
	lame	shake	rail

rain	snaily	trainers	grey
sails	tail	wail	they
snail	trail	wait	
snails	train		

(Words containing sounds and spellings practised in the Blue and Green Storybooks and the other Purple Storybooks have been used in the story, too.)

Other words

Also included are some common words (e.g. **little**, **your**) which your child will be learning in his or her first few years at school.

A few other words have been used to help the story to flow.

Reading the book

1 Make sure you and your child are sitting in a quiet, comfortable place.

2 Tell him or her a little about the story, without giving too much away:

Jake goes to the Crazy Ape theme park - and ends up whizzing round the world on the back of a snail!

This will give your child a mental picture; having a context for a story makes it easier to read the words.

3 Read the target words (above) together. This will mean that you can both enjoy the story without having to spend too much time working out the words. Help your child to sound out each word (e.g. **s-n-ai-l**) before saying the whole word.

4 Let your child read the story aloud. Help him or her with any difficult words and discuss the story as you go along. Stop now and again to ask your child to predict what will happen next. This will help you to see whether he or she has understood what has happened so far.

Above all, enjoy the story, and praise your child's reading!

Ruth Miskin's

Superphonics

Purple Storybook

The
Runaway Snail

by Gill Munton

Illustrated by Clive Scruton

Hodder
Children's
Books

a division of Hodder Headline Limited

It's the very first day of the holiday,

And Jake's got a brand new game

   to play,

But now he's looking for

   something new:

"I'm bored, I'm bored,

   there's nothing to do!"

"Okay," says Dad,

"I give up, I give in!

We'll take an awayday, Jake,

you win!

The Crazy Ape is the place to go -

It's the very latest thing, you know!"

They pay at the gate,
and go into the park.

First, the ghost train – dim and dark!
Spooks with chains that chink
and shake,
And frighten the life out of Dad
(but not Jake).

Dad's face is green, and a little pale,

As banshees bay and witches wail.

Next, a pale and ghostly shape –

"That's IT!" says Dad,
  as he tries to escape.

"For goodness sake! It's just a ride!

Shut your eyes till we get outside!"

"That's the last ride I go on today.

You're on your own! Just go away!"

"Come on, come on,

this way, this way

To the biggest thrill you'll have today!

You'll want to ride again and again

On the megafantastic Snail Train!"

Jake is pulled, as if by a thread

To a big black snail,

   with a big grey head.

"Black is his shell,

   and grey is his tail –

This is what I CALL a snail!"

Jake gets on, and the snails glide

Round the track to the end of the ride.

But when they get to the boating lake,

Jake's snail begins to hum and shake ...

And takes off at an amazing rate

Along the rail – and out of the gate!

"Stop! Wait! Stop that snail!"

(Jake's hanging on tight,

His face pale green,

and his knuckles white.)

"I'm afraid you've made a big mistake!
Did you forget to put on the brake?"

But the snail gains speed
   with a whizz and a whirr,
And the Crazy Ape flashes by
   in a blur.

"You lame-brained snail,

 you're not in a race!

But wait a sec – what IS this place?
A plate of snails ... a Metro train ...
It must be Paris, in the rain!"

Jake hears a yell, and turns to gape ...

"It's all the kids from the Crazy Ape!"

Some on skateboards, some on bikes,
Some in trainers, or running spikes.

"We're on your trail, your snaily trail,

Your grimy, slimy, snaily trail!

Along the shiny silver rail,

We're on the trail of the runaway snail!"

"You can't catch me –

I'm afraid you'll fail,

However much you weep and wail.

You may as well chase the Holy Grail

As chase the amazing runaway snail!"

And with this cry,

the snail-with-no-shame

Glides into a place of worldwide fame –

The very heart of the city of Rome!

But:

"Stop that snail! I want to go home!"

The snail sails on,

   like an express train,

Or even a supersonic plane!

(This must be a case of snail rage.

I think we'd better turn the page.)

"We're on your trail, your snaily trail,

Your grimy, slimy, snaily trail!

Along the shiny silver rail,

We're on the trail of the runaway snail!"

"You can't catch me –

I'm afraid you'll fail,

However much you weep and wail.

You may as well chase the Holy Grail

As chase the amazing runaway snail!"

"Just wait," says Jake, "I haven't paid
To be in a fancy dress parade!

I just wanted to ride the Snail Train,

Not go round the world,

    again and again!"

But the snail is rumbling to a halt.

"I'm sorry, mate! It was all my fault!

I've got to go home –

   I've run out of juice!

(And I think my shell is getting loose!)

I didn't mean to make you late.

I'll soon have you back at the

   Crazy Ape gate."

Jake said to the snail, "I'm very glad.

And by the way - I can see my Dad!

And after today,

we're BOTH going to stay

Away from the Crazy Ape - okay?"